Señor Smarty Pantaloons and the Mystery of the Missing Teachers

Written by
Regina Davis;Carolyn Royer Spencer

Illustrated by Carolyn Royer Spencer

Regina Davis was born and raised in Long Island, New York and now lives in Virginia Beach. She received her B.S. in Elementary Education from St. John's University and her M.A. from Hofstra. Regina was Reading Teacher of the Year at Newtown Road Elementary in Virginia Beach and is a member of the International Reading Association. She enjoys writing poetry and her poem, "Tomorrow" , was published in "Across the Universe" in 1996. After teaching elementary school for 37 years in New York and Virginia, she recently retired. Her hobbies are reading, writing, and travel. She loves animals, especially cats!

Carolyn Royer Spencer is a lifetime resident of Norfolk, Virginia. She received her B.S. in Art and her B.S. certification in Early Childhood and Elementary Education from Old Dominion University. Carolyn taught kindergarten, Title 1 kindergarten, first and second grades for almost thirty years in Norfolk and Virginia Beach and served as a career teacher. She is a member of the International Reading Association. Her hobbies include golf and travel. This quote expresses Carolyn's view on children and art: "My favorite thing about children is their individual creativity! I love to see children create their own style of art with such ease and enjoyment."

AuthorHouse™
1663 Liberty Drive
Bloomington, IN 47403
www.authorhouse.com
Phone: 1 (800) 839-8640

Published by AuthorHouse 01/04/2017

ISBN: 978-1-4567-4557-8 (sc)
ISBN: 978-1-5246-5354-5 (hc)
ISBN: 978-1-4772-0127-5 (e)

Library of Congress Control Number: 2011902994

Print information available on the last page.

Any people depicted in stock imagery provided by Thinkstock are models, and such images are being used for illustrative purposes only. Certain stock imagery © Thinkstock.

This book is printed on acid-free paper.

Because of the dynamic nature of the Internet, any web addresses or links contained in this book may have changed since publication and may no longer be valid. The views expressed in this work are solely those of the author and do not necessarily reflect the views of the publisher, and the publisher hereby disclaims any responsibility for them.

authorHOUSE®

Dedication

Carolyn Royer Spencer dedicates this book to her son, David William Spencer, for his creative inspiration. Special mention goes to her granddaughter, Leah Elizabeth DeCarlis.

Regina Davis dedicates this book to her granddaughter, Kalila Danisi, who aspires to be an author someday. Special mention goes to her grandson, Deven Danisi.

Things got really out of control last spring at Foxaloon Elementary School. It all started when Principal Foxanna Powerpaws announced on the loudspeaker that Mrs. Sheila Sheepshank, Teacher of the Year, should come to the office at her lunch hour.

All of the students thought that the wise Mrs. Sheepshank was probably about to receive another award. However, they knew that was not the case when the powerful Miss Powerpaws started screaming at old, shy Sheila Sheepshank! Mrs. Sheepshank was in BIG trouble with the principal, but why? While all of the other students just wondered, sneaky Iradella listened at the door of the principal's office. All she could hear was that Mrs. Sheepshank had lost a special library book. Why would that make Miss Powerpaws so angry?

The next day Mrs. Sheepshank didn't come to work. She'd never been absent before. Mrs. Patricia Giraffic, the school secretary, kept phoning Mrs. Sheepshank to find out if she was sick, but there was no answer.

At 11:30 a.m., Miss Powerpaws announced on the loudspeaker that the math teacher, Mr. Muttonmouth, should report to her office at lunchtime. The elderly, marvelous Mr. Muttonmouth was such an awesome teacher that the students just knew that he was about to be awarded a special math prize! However, they soon found out that was not what was happening!

After he entered the principal's office, the powerful Miss Powerpaws pounced on him! Naughty Nadena put her ear to the keyhole and learned that Mr. Muttonmouth was being scolded for losing a ruler. Why would that make Miss Powerpaws so angry? To make things even stranger, Mr. Muttonmouth did not come to school the next day!

It was a dark, stormy Wednesday, and it was raining cats and dogs, but all of the teachers came to work, except Mrs. Sheepshank and Mr. Muttonmouth. They had somehow disappeared after being yelled at by the principal. Which teacher would be next to face Miss Powerpaws? Nosy, know-it-all Nolton listened in at the office door and overheard that both Mrs. Lana Lambo and Miss Myrtle Merino had misplaced their classroom door keys. Miss Powerpaws was furious with them. Would Lana Lambo and Myrtle Merino vanish into thin air like the others had?

Everyone was anxious to get to Foxaloon Elementary on Thursday morning. As most of the teachers had feared, two more teachers were missing! The situation had now turned into a real mystery. The secretary called the police. "It's a missing persons emergency!" she shouted. The police conducted a search of the school building and all the missing teachers' homes, but they were nowhere to be found! What happened to the four missing teachers?

Principal Foxanna Powerpaws had put on weight recently. Could this be a clue to the sudden disappearance of the four older teachers? Had Miss Powerpaws eaten them? Some students went to Señor Smarty Pantaloons, the school's robotic computer, to ask his opinion. He shouted, "Opinions don't count because opinions aren't facts!" More calmly, he added, "However, it's a fact that foxes eat sheep. Sheep are their prey." The worried students decided to keep on looking for the missing teachers. It was just too awful to imagine that the principal might have eaten them!

Over the weekend, know-it-all Nolton told his grandparents, who were visiting from out of town, all about the missing teachers at his school. His grandfather, Cool G. Daddy Big Dwayne, said, "I doubt that the principal would have eaten them. Perhaps they met the same fate as the older teachers at Wolverton Woods Elementary School." Nolton asked, "What happened to them, G. Daddy?"

G. Daddy replied, "Most older teachers earn more jellybeans than younger teachers do. Miss Wolverina Woollyclaws, the principal of Wolverton Woods Elementary, came up with an idea last year. She wanted the older teachers to leave her school so that she wouldn't have to give away as many jellybeans. She could then trade the extra jellybeans for school supplies." Nolton thought, *Oh, no! Could Miss Powerpaws have been so sly and greedy that she caused those four fine missing teachers to leave their students? Then she could barter their jellybeans for a robotic computer, like Señor Smarty Pantaloons!*

As soon as he arrived at school on Monday morning, Nolton asked Señor Smarty Pantaloons, "Did Miss Powerpaws trade the extra jellybeans that she saved by getting rid of those four missing teachers so that she could get you?"

Señor Smarty Pantaloons responded, "Yes! That kind of trading is called bartering. Let me give you one important clue. If they're not earning jellybeans at Foxaloon Elementary, those teachers must be working somewhere else."

Miss Sheepshoe, Nolton's teacher, heard the brilliant robotic computer's reply. She said, "He's right, as usual. We just need to find where those teachers have jobs now, but students, right now your job is to turn on your laptops for Señor Smarty Pantaloons' morning assignment!"

Nolton could hardly wait for the school day to end so that he could search for the missing teachers there. As soon as he arrived home, he jumped on G. Daddy's skateboard and rounded up all of the kids in the neighborhood. They spent countless hours searching the town of Foxaloon, but didn't find the beloved teachers. Nolton arrived home at 8:00 p.m., sweaty, hungry, and disappointed, but he thought to himself, *Maybe tomorrow there will be a crack in the case of the missing teachers!*

Cool G. Daddy Big Dwayne likes to skate every day. One day he was skating around the largest farm in nearby Lionsrock, when, to his surprise, he spotted the four missing teachers with their hooves against a fence! G. Daddy said, "Ooooh, my! I can't believe my eyes! You have been let out to pasture, and it looks as if you have been sheared! Why are you here?"

Mrs. Sheepshank pointed her hoof at a quaint old shop, behind the barn. Crotchety Crow's Knitting Nook sold all sorts of woolen items. She told G. Daddy, "We're trading our wool for food. The Knitting Nook sells scarves and mittens that are made from wool."

Weeping quietly, Mr. Muttonmouth added, "We all miss our students. How are they doing without us?"

G. Daddy answered, "You don't deserve to have been put out to pasture like this!"

Mrs. Sheepshank said, "We mustn't return to school until we find the missing book, ruler, and keys."

"Don't worry," said G. Daddy. "Señor Smarty Pantaloons found those missing items. They were under Miss Powerpaws's desk! It is now safe for you to go back. The students all miss you so much! I will open the gate so that you can return to Foxaloon Elementary School after spring break!"

As always, Señor Smarty Pantaloons had come to the rescue!

Señor Smarty Pantaloons,
Wearing pantaloons of gray,
Always to the rescue
With his cosmic, high-tech ways!